A Fairy in the family!

By
Avril O'Reilly

ISBN 978-1-4092-8061-3

9 781409 280613

Dedicated
to the
Patterson Family

The Greens were a very lucky family.

Their daughter Bekki was a real fairy!

Dad, Mum, brother Sam and Humphrey the dog and Fluffypuff the cat were all normal but Bekki was special.

She could do magic spells!

Bekki was a very pretty fairy with a big, bright, happy smile.

She had a big smile because she had spent the morning casting spells for her whole family.

There was just one problem...

Bekki noticed that today she was looking rather odd.

She had dishcloth wings, cheesy wellies instead of silk slippers and feather dusters where her tutu should be.

There was rubbish in her hair and a mouse living in her left welly. Worst of all, every time she waved her wand it went "BLURPP!!!".

It would be fair to say, Bekki was a bit of a mess.

Squeak

All the other fairies looked neat and tidy. When they waved their wands it sounded like the tinkling of tiny bells.
They had no rubbish in their hair

and their wands certainly didn't go "BLURP!!!".

Now this made Bekki very sad. Most little girls like to look as nice as their friends and this is especially true of little girls who do magic.

Bekki decided to go and see Natalie the Head Fairy.

Off Bekki flew to see Natalie, the Head Fairy.

WHOOOSH!

Whenever Bekki had a fairy problem, Natalie would always sort it out.

Natalie was beautiful with kind brown eyes, a floaty, sparkling dress and a sliver of golden light for her wand.

When she waved her wand it sounded like the whistling of a tiny flute. She had no junk in her hair and her wand certainly didn't go "BLURP!!".

"Excuuuuuse me !",
said Bekki,

"but why do all the other
fairies look nicer than me?"

"It's all to do with your magic", explained Natalie the Head Fairy.

Tiny stars glittered and danced around her wand as she spoke.

"You had a beautiful fairy outfit this morning but each time you did a naughty spell your outfit changed."

Bekki thought about what the Head Fairy had said. She looked at her wand – a toilet brush covered in globs of bright pink bubblegum.

It looked like a naughty wand, but why?

Bekki was confused.

"Me? Naughty spells? Me? I don't remember doing any naughty spells Head Fairy."

"Remember, remember,
cast your mind back,"
said Natalie,

"you used to have a beautiful
pink skirt...until..."

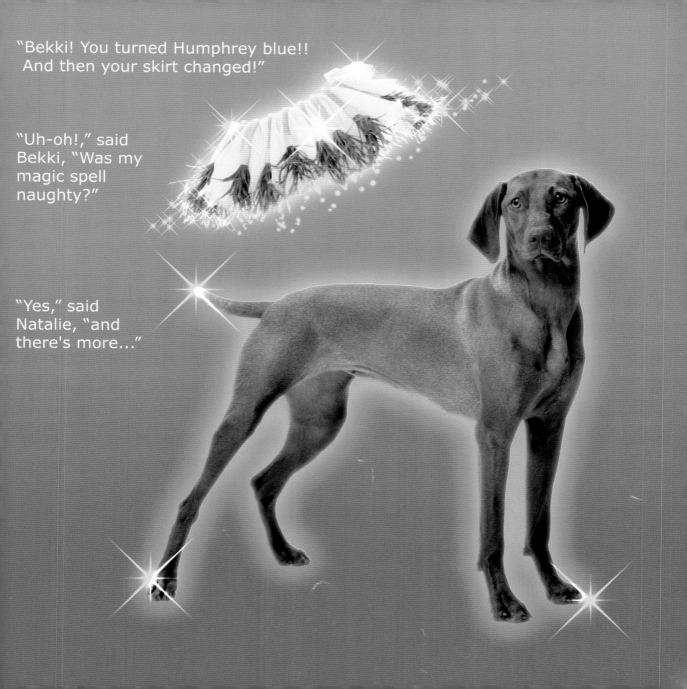

"Bekki! You turned Humphrey blue!! And then your skirt changed!"

"Uh-oh!," said Bekki, "Was my magic spell naughty?"

"Yes," said Natalie, "and there's more..."

"Remember, remember, cast your mind back.

You used to have wonderful pink

slippers...until..."

"Bekki! You turned your Dad's shoes into clown boots! And then your silk slippers turned into cheesy wellies!"

"Uh-oh!," said Bekki, "Was that magic spell naughty too?"

"Yes," said Natalie, "and there's more..."

"Remember, remember, cast your mind back.

You used to have a splendid tiara with sparkles and jewels...until..."

"Bekki! You shrank your Mum's washing machine!!
And then your tiara turned into rubbish!"

"Uh-oh!," said Bekki, "Was that magic spell naughty too?"

"Yes," said Natalie, "and there's more..."

"Remember, remember, cast your mind back.

You used to have a fabulous shimmering wand...until..."

Bekki thought about how all her spells had ruined her beautiful fairy outfit.

"Well, excuuuuse me!," she said ,

"I thought everyone would be pleased with such fun spells."

Bekki took out her toilet brush wand and thought of a new spell.

"BLUUURP!!!"

In a big flash of magic Bekki undid all her naughty spells.

Look!

"Oh Bekki!

Look at you now, You're beautiful again!" said Natalie the Head Fairy.

Bekki was the prettiest fairy of them all.

"Thank you, Head Fairy," said Bekki, "No more naughty spells for me!"

"But... poor Fluffypuff looks a little boring. I'll do a spell to cheer her up!"

"BLURP!"

"Oh Bekki, Bekki, Bekki...."

Remember! Remember! Cast your mind back!

How many good fairies are there?

What colour are Mum's frilly pants?

What is Bekki's naughty wand made of?

Does Sam turn into a banana, a hotdog or a strawberry?

What lives in Bekki's cheesy welly?

Are Dad's clown boots stripy or spotty?

Who is Fluffypuff?

What sound does Bekki's wand make?

What colour is Natalie's dress?

'A Fairy in the family' is available on
www.amazon.com
and
www.lulu.com

Thanks to:

Chanelle Alexander, Jennifer Alford, Allyson Allman, Zaakirah Basil,
The Bead Shop in Covent Garden,
Madame de Belle, Ozwald Boateng, Broadwick Silks,
Bruce and Brown London Kids, Chris Bowden,
Sapphire Buckingham, Steve Caplin, Dr Anne Cremona,
Essence, Getty Images, Larry Lamptey, Dr Sue Mack,
Bruce Mackie, Microtextiles in Willesden, Ingrid Molinos,
Nathalie Mohoboob, Carol Morley at Frank, Diane O'Reilly,
Gertie O'Reilly, Ava Tennant, Tom O'Reilly, Adam Parker,
Tabatha Parker, Tony Robbins, V.V. Rouleaux ,
Paul Strutt at Angels, Caroline Shearing, Elisabeth Smith,
James Taylor at Tough Little Graphic, David J Thomas School Outfitters,
Emmeline Webster, Sam Webster, Wear Moi,
Venita at Future Matters Consultancy, Verna Wilkins, Woolworths.

And of course to Tolani Lambo,
who has always been the heart and soul of the project.